# A HOLIDAY FOR
## ~ The ~
## THREE BEARS

*For Stephanie*
*T.B.*

First published in Great Britain in hardback
by HarperCollins Publishers Ltd in 1995
10 9 8 7 6 5 4 3 2 1
First published in Picture Lions in 1995
10 9 8 7 6 5 4 3 2 1
Picture Lions is an imprint of the Children's Division,
part of HarperCollins Publishers Ltd.
Text copyright © Tony Bradman 1995
Illustrations copyright © Jenny Williams 1995
A CIP catalogue record for this title is available from the British Library.
The author and illustrator assert the moral right
to be identified as the author and illustrator of the work.
ISBN: 0 00 193890-8 (hardback)
0 00 664333-7 (Picture Lions)

Produced by HarperCollins Hong Kong
This book is set in Caslon 540

# A HOLIDAY FOR
## ~ The ~
# THREE BEARS

### TONY BRADMAN & JENNY WILLIAMS

## PictureLions

*An Imprint of HarperCollinsPublishers*

Sunday evening at the Bears' House
Finds the three of them quite glum;
What a weekend! What disasters!
Father's brain was almost numb.

Junior had been a terror,
And they'd had a burglary;
Goldilocks had wrecked the cottage,
Then escaped, so easily.

Father read the *Forest Bugle:*
" *'Leave your worries all behind...*
*We've a welcome waiting for you!*
*We can offer peace of mind.*

*Come to friendly Transylvania!*
*Take a break... woods, lakes and sun...'*
That's the ticket. It sounds perfect.
Just the place to have some fun!"

Mother phoned to make the booking,
They could go, within a week!
Junior was *so* excited
That for once he couldn't speak.

Soon the Bears were very busy,
There was such a lot to pack.
Junior added things he needed.
Mother made him put some back.

It was hectic at the airport.
They were told of long delays.
Mother spoke to one young couple
Who had waited several days.

Then at last their plane was ready.
Mother strapped in Junior tight.
Father now felt very nervous.
He hoped for a nice, smooth flight.

But the weather was appalling,
And poor Father looked quite ill.
Junior lent him pen and paper
So he could make out his will.

Hours later they descended,
With a bump came into land,
Disembarked with all the others,
Listened to a local band,

And discovered that their luggage
Hadn't been put on the plane.
Mother asked a lot of questions.
Junior was a little pain.

Father said it didn't matter.
"Now our holiday's begun
We should just *ignore* such troubles.
We've arrived, let's have some fun!"

They were picked up by a carriage
With a driver dressed in black.
Off they went into the mountains.
Junior loved the whiplash crack.

Over bridges, through a village,
Past a church with tolling bell.
Shadows lengthened and the moon rose.
Then they saw it... their hotel.

Father said he thought it charming.
Mother wasn't quite so sure.
Lightning flashed, they heard a creaking;
Someone opened up the door.

"Welcome to my humble castle,"
Said The Count, "just walk this way."
He was strange, but very friendly.
Hoped they'd have a pleasant stay.

"Igor, show our guests their chambers.
Don't forget – you dine at eight.
Please excuse me, I must fly now.
I'm already rather late."

Up the stairs they followed Igor,
To some dark and gloomy rooms.
Mother didn't like the decor,
Said she'd seen more cheery tombs.

She went off to check the bathroom.
Junior peered into a chest
Which contained old bits and pieces.
Could this be a former guest?

Father looked out of the window,
Planning his pre-breakfast run.
"I can feel myself relaxing,
And I *know* we'll have some fun."

Later on they went to dinner,
Igor showed them where to sit.
Someone chanted in the kitchen:
"Hubble, bubble, blood and spit..."

Igor and the staff were busy,
There were lots of hungry guests.
Soon Junior was being naughty
With two other little pests.

Father didn't take much notice;
He was worried by the food.
Mother ate some for politeness;
Trying nothing would be rude.

After dinner they were tired,
Junior's mood, in fact, was foul.
Somewhere in the nearby forest
They could hear a creature howl.

Father cuddled up to Mother.
He was feeling rather scared.
Just above them was a portrait
With two eyes that glowed and stared.

In the morning Father jumped up,
Woken by the golden sun.
He felt fresh and fit and healthy;
"Come on dear, let's have some fun!"

But poor Mother lay there groaning.
She had suffered in the night;
What she'd eaten had upset her.
She wished she'd been less polite.

Father said he'd be back shortly.
Out he went to have his jog.
It was pleasant in the forest...
Till he met a large, fierce dog.

Father didn't stop to argue.
He ran fast, and no mistake.
Had his breakfast, checked on Mother,
Then took Junior to the lake.

It was peaceful in the sunshine
And the gentle, balmy breeze...
But the calm was swiftly shattered
By someone on water-skis.

Junior was quite delighted
By the things that he'd seen done;
Then said Father ought to try it.
"Well, why not? Let's have some fun!"

Father thought it was amazing.
Then he glimpsed some sharp teeth flash...
He forgot what he was doing,
Landed with an awful crash.

Father limped back, looking battered,
Had a lie-down for a while.
Mother now was feeling better.
Junior's story made her smile.

Later, Junior was invited
To a club where he could play
With the other little children
Who were there on holiday.

Painting pictures kept him busy,
And he got a nice surprise.
Igor ran a competition –
Junior won a mystery prize.

Igor said he'd send the prize on
To the Bears when they were home.
Junior wrote down where to post it
In an ancient, dusty tome.

Dinner time came all too quickly;
Mother took one look... and fled.
Something on her plate was moving.
Igor came and shot it dead.

BANG!

Junior, of course, was naughty,
Then a crowd came to the door,
Asking Igor where The Count was;
"String him up!" they yelled, and swore.

"Time for bed, I think," said Mother.
And they went straight to their room.
Outside there were screams, and shouting.
Torchlight flickered in the gloom.

After midnight, things went quiet.
Then they heard a squeaky peep.
Something flew in through the window...
So they didn't get much sleep.

In the morning they decided
To conclude their holiday.
Father got the bill from Igor.
It was quite a lot to pay.

Soon they'd packed and joined the carriage
With that driver dressed in black.
Off they went, down from the mountains,
Glad that they were going back.

At the airport it was hectic,
They were told of long delays.
Father spoke to one young couple
Who had been there several days.

Then at last their plane was ready.
Up above, the sun shone bright...
But in minutes storm clouds gathered,
And they had an *awful* flight.

It was raining when they got home.

All three were in gloomy mood.

Downstairs was completely flooded

And they didn't have much food.

But next morning bright and early
Junior got a big surprise.
Igor had sent him a letter,
Giving details of his prize.

*'Please return to Transylvania!*
*You have won... free holiday!*
*Here are tickets. P.S. Luggage*
*Got to castle yesterday!'*

Mother sat there, hardly moving,
And her face was full of pain.
Muttering, she shook the letter.
"We're not going *there* again."

Junior then suggested something;
Both his parents were impressed.
As an idea, it was brilliant.
Suddenly, they weren't depressed.

They sat down and wrote a letter,
Telling Goldilocks she'd won
Two whole weeks in Transylvania,
Where she would have *lots of fun*.

So our story ends in laughter;
Each Bear wears a joyful smile.
They'll live happy ever after...
Well, at least just for a while!

Have you read the

Bears' first adventure?

A BAD WEEK FOR

THE THREE BEARS

# Here are some more Picture Lions

**BADGER'S PARTING GIFTS**
Susan Varley

Quentin Blake
**MISTER MAGNOLIA**

**KATIE MORAG AND THE TIRESOME TED**
Mairi Hedderwick

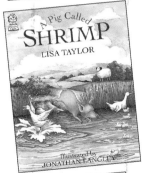

A Pig Called **SHRIMP**
LISA TAYLOR
Illustrated by JONATHAN LANGLEY

**A BAD WEEK FOR The THREE BEARS**
TONY BRADMAN & JENNY WILLIAMS

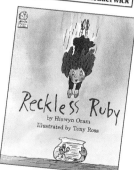

**Reckless Ruby**
by Hiawyn Oram
Illustrated by Tony Ross

**Monsters**
Colin & Jacqui Hawkins

**WHERE THE WILD THINGS ARE**
STORY AND PICTURES BY MAURICE SENDAK

Michael Rosen & Quentin Blake
**DON'T** Put Mustard in the Custard

## for you to enjoy